Farm Machines At Work

Tractors

By Hal Rogers

The Child's World® Inc.

Published by The Child's World®, Inc.

Design and Production:
The Creative Spark, San Juan Capistrano, CA

Photos: © 1999 David M. Budd Photography

Library of Congress Cataloging-in-Publication Data

Rogers, Hal
      Tractors / by Hal Rogers.
          p. cm.
      Summary: Simple text describes the parts of a tractor, how they work, and what they do.
      ISBN 1-56766-752-X (lib. bdg.)
      1. Farm tractors—Juvenile literature. [1. Tractors. 2. Agricultural machinery.] I. Title.

    S711 .R57 2000
    631.3'72--dc21

                                                      99-089468

Contents

On the Job

On the job, farmers use tractors to work in their fields.

This tractor has a big **blade** on the front of it. The farmer uses the blade to push things out of the way.

The blade can push animal **feed** into

a neat pile. If it snows, the blade can

push snow off roads, too.

Some tractors have big wheels.

Other tractors have **crawler tracks.**

The wheels and crawler tracks

help tractors move across rough,

bumpy fields.

A tractor can pull heavy machines, such as a **plow.** A plow helps get **soil** ready for planting.

A tractor can also pull a **trailer.**

Trailers can carry **grain** from the

field to a **silo.**

Farmers have used tractors for many years. Today's tractors look very different from older ones.

Climb Aboard!

Do you want to see where the farmer sits? The field is very dusty. The **cab** protects the farmer from dust. The farmer uses a steering wheel to drive the tractor. The farmer uses **controls** to run machines that the tractor pulls.

Up Close

The inside

1. The controls

2. The steering wheel

3. The driver's seat

The outside

1. The blade

2. The wheels

3. The cab

4. The crawler tracks

Glossary

blade (BLAYD)
A blade is a sharp metal tool on the front of a tractor. A blade pushes things out of the way.

cab (KAB)
A cab is where a farmer sits to drive a tractor. A cab has a seat, a steering wheel, and controls.

controls (kun-TROLZ)
Controls are tools that are used to help make something work. A farmer uses controls to run the machines that a tractor pulls.

crawler tracks (KRAH-ler TRAX)
Crawler tracks are huge belts that run around and around to move a machine back and forth. Some tractors have crawler tracks.

feed (FEED)
Feed is food for animals. A tractor blade can push feed into a pile.

grain (GRANE)
Grain is food that comes from the seeds of grassy plants. Grain provides food for people and animals.

plow (PLOW)
A plow is a machine that can be pulled by a tractor. A plow turns soil over and breaks it up.

silo (SY-loh)
A silo is a tall, round building on a farm. Farmers store grain or feed in silos.

soil (SOYL)
Soil is the dirt in a field or garden. A plow gets soil ready for planting.

trailer (TRAY-ler)
A trailer is a vehicle that is used to carry things. A trailer can be pulled by a tractor or other vehicle.